I Love to Write!

I write a list when I want to bake.

Dear Sarah,
I am having so much fun! I go swimming every day! I can't wait to go fishing, too.
Your friend,
Anne

Sarah Kim
323 Hill Road
Baytown, WI
20343

I write a postcard when I'm at the lake.

I write in my journal every day.

I write when I have something important to say.

I write a card
just to say hello.

I write a report
about what I know.

I write a note
when I'll be late.

I write when I want
to communicate!

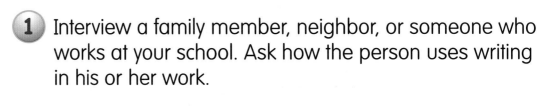

1. Interview a family member, neighbor, or someone who works at your school. Ask how the person uses writing in his or her work.

2. Make a list of all the ways you used writing in the past month. Share your list with classmates, and make a class poster.

Room 12 Writes!
We write in our journals.
We write about our garden.
We write letters to our Star of the Week.
We write about our field trip.